W9-CAT-664

Graphic design and illustrations: Zapp
Story adaptation: Jane Brierley

© 1995 Tormont Publications Inc.
  338 Saint Antoine St. East
  Montreal, Canada H2Y 1A3
  Tel. (514) 954-1441
  Fax (514) 954-5086

ISBN 2-89429-850-1

Printed in China

SLEEPING BEAUTY

TORMONT

Once upon a time, there lived a king and queen who longed for a child. One day, as the queen was brushing her hair, a little frog jumped off his lily pad and onto the queen's windowsill.

"You will soon become a mother," the frog croaked.

6

Some months later, just before the sun peeped over the mountains, a little princess was born.

The king and queen were overjoyed. "Our daughter is as beautiful as the rosy morning sky!" the king cried. "We'll call her Aurora, since that's another name for the dawn."

"We must have a very special christening," said the queen. "We'll invite all the lords and ladies of the kingdom, and all the fairy folk, too."

The king's messengers were soon sent far and wide to deliver the invitations.

At last the great day dawned. Even before the lords and ladies began to arrive, the twelve good fairies of the kingdom came gliding through the air. "All the fairies are coming!" cried the happy queen. But there was a thirteenth fairy — a fairy who had *not* been invited.

9

At the christening feast, the table glittered with gold plates. Baby Aurora lay in a beautiful cradle in the middle of the banquet hall.

When the feast was nearly over, the good fairies flew up to the cradle, one by one, and made a special wish as a gift.

"Let her be wise," said one. "May she know the truest love," said the next. Just as the eleventh fairy flew away from the cradle, a gust of wind blew out the candles. Suddenly, the dark hall was lit by a burst of lightning and black smoke. A terrible figure flew over the cradle. The thirteenth fairy!

"So, I'm not good enough to be invited to this baby's christening!" shrieked the wicked fairy. "I have a wish for her, all the same. On her sixteenth birthday, may she prick her finger on a spindle and die!"

With a terrible cackle, the wicked fairy disappeared. The king and queen knelt beside the cradle. "How were we to know there was a thirteenth fairy?" sobbed the queen.

At that moment, the twelfth fairy flew up to the cradle.

"I still have a wish for the princess," she said gently. "The thirteenth fairy's power is great. I can't break her spell, but I can soften it."

She waved her wand and exclaimed for all to hear, "When the princess pricks her finger, she will not die, but will sleep for a hundred years, to be awakened by the kiss of true love."

The king was grateful, but he took no chances. He ordered that every spinning wheel in the kingdom be burned.

The princess grew up to be a lovely young woman. On the day of her sixteenth birthday, everyone in the castle was busy preparing for the celebration.

"Run along, my dear," said the queen to Aurora. "We'll call you when it's time." Aurora decided to explore one of the castle towers. Up, up she went. At last, she came to a big door.

The princess turned the rusty key and
pushed open the door. What a strange
sight met her eyes! On a pile of wool in a
corner beside a cot, sat an old woman
beside a strange object.

"Hello," said the princess shyly. "What are you doing?"

"Why, my dear, I'm spinning wool thread," said the old woman. "This is a spinning wheel, and here's the spindle." And as she spoke, her fingers twisted the thread and rolled it quickly onto the spindle. "Would you like to try?"

"Oh yes!" said Aurora excitedly. The old woman smiled and handed her the spindle, point first. There was a flash of light and the sound of wicked laughter as the princess pricked her finger and fainted onto the cot.

The twelfth good fairy had been keeping
watch. She knew that the wicked fairy's
evil spell had partly worked, and that the
princess lay in a deep sleep.

Now, she quickly flew about the castle,
waving her wand and casting a spell over
everyone and everything in it.

People and animals fell asleep in the middle of whatever they were doing. The clocks stopped ticking, and time itself seemed to stand still in the castle.

Outside, thorny bushes poked up from the ground. As the weeks went by, they became taller and taller until you couldn't even see the castle towers behind them.

With time, the castle was gradually forgotten. Sometimes an old grandfather would tell a tale of the Sleeping Beauty who lay within a thorn-covered castle waiting for the kiss of true love.

The years rolled by. From time to time,
adventurous young men set out to free the
mysterious princess from her deep sleep.
They tried to cut through the
towering hedge of thorns, but before long
they were forced to turn back. The thorns
tore at the poor horses' legs, and the
branches seemed to reach out to trip them.

At the end of a hundred years, almost no one remembered the story of the sleeping princess. The towering hedge was now a thorny forest.

One day, a young prince named Mikail came to a nearby village. As he was talking to the villagers, an old man asked, "Have you ever known true love, my son?"

"No," said the prince, "but I long to."

"You're just the man to wake our Sleeping Beauty!" the old man cried, and he told Prince Mikail about the legend.

The prince rode off to the thorny forest, feeling sure a great adventure awaited him. Now, this was the very day of the princess's sixteenth birthday, a hundred years ago. As he entered the forest, the prickly branches became as limp as seaweed, and his horse passed through unharmed.

As Prince Mikail rode up to the castle, he saw dozens of dogs and horses frozen in sleep.

"How curious," he said to himself. "This must truly be an enchanted place."

Inside the great hall, he found the king and queen and all the courtiers and servants dozing just where they had fallen asleep so long ago. On and on he went, until at last he opened the door at the top of the tower.

There, on a small cot, lay the princess. The prince fell to his knees beside Sleeping Beauty and gazed at her. A new feeling had entered his heart. "This must be true love," he thought. He gently lifted her hand and kissed it.

At that moment, Princess Aurora opened her eyes and smiled at Prince Mikail.

Downstairs, the castle sprang to life. The cat jumped up and began to chase a mouse. In the doorways, the guards rubbed their eyes. The dogs stood up and barked. Servants began running back and forth as they had done a hundred years ago, getting ready for the princess's birthday.

"My, how dusty everything looks!" exclaimed the queen.

"Never mind, my dear," said the king, yawning and stretching. "By the time our guests go home, it will be a lot dustier!"

"Oh dear, I must tell Aurora to hurry!" said the queen. But as she spoke, the princess was carried in by a handsome stranger. "My darling!" cried the queen, hurrying over to her. She took her daughter's hand and saw the spindle scar.

Just then, the good fairies arrived and told
the king and queen what had happened.
"You have broken the wicked fairy's spell!"
the king cried, smiling at the prince.

And so the prince and princess found
true love, and lived happily ever after.